"For if you forgive men when they sin against
your heavenly Father will also forgive you."

—Matthew 6:14

ZONDERKIDZ

The Berenstain Bears® and the Forgiving Tree
Copyright © 2010 by Berenstain Publishing, Inc.
Illustrations © 2010 by Berenstain Publishing, Inc.

Requests for information should be addressed to:
Zonderkidz, 3900 *Sparks Dr. SE, Grand Rapids, Michigan* 49546

Library of Congress Cataloging-in-Publication Data

Berenstain, Jan, 1923–
        The Berenstain Bears and the forgiving tree / by Jan and Mike Berenstain.
            p.   cm.
        ISBN 978-0-310-72084-3 (softcover)
        [1. Birthdays—Fiction. 2. Parties—Fiction. 3. Forgiveness—Fiction. 4. Bears—Fiction. 5.
Christian life—Fiction.] I. Berenstain, Michael. II. The Berenstain Bears and the Forgiving Tree.
PZ7.B44826Bd   2011
[E]—dc22   2010009502

Editor: Mary Hassinger
Art direction: Cindy Davis

Printed in China

16 17 18 19 20 21 22 23 24 25 /DSC/ 23 22 21 20 19 18 17 16 15 14 13

The Berenstain Bears®

The FORGIVING TREE

Living Lights™
A Faith Story

ZONDERkidz

It was a special day in a tree house down a sunny dirt road deep in Bear Country. It was Brother Bear's birthday.

"Happy Birthday, Brother!" shouted the party guests as Mama brought in the cake. Then they all sang the birthday song.

"Make a wish!" said Sister.
Brother closed his eyes, made a wish, and blew out the candles.
"YEA!" the guests yelled, clapping and blowing on noisemakers.

Papa cut the cake and everyone dug in.
"What did you wish for?" asked Cousin Fred.
"If I tell, it won't come true," said Brother.

When they were finished eating the cake, it was time to open presents. Brother got some very nice ones—a model plane, some books, a racing car set, and a video game.

Then he noticed Papa sneaking into the next room. When he came back, he was pushing ... *a brand-new bike!*

"Wow!" said Brother excitedly. "It's exactly what I wished for!"

"Lucky you didn't tell Fred," said Sister.

"That's a beautiful bike," said Fred, admiring it. "I sure wish I had a bike like that."

"Oh," said Brother, without thinking, "you can borrow it anytime you like."

"Gee, thanks!" said Fred.

"Let's try out your new video game," suggested Sister.

All the cubs crowded around while Brother and Sister played the new video game. They were so interested, they didn't notice anything else for awhile. But then Brother looked over at his brand-new bike. It was gone!

"Hey!" said Brother. "Where's my new bike?"

"Say," said Lizzy, looking out the window, "isn't that Fred riding it?"

Lizzy was right. Cousin Fred was outside riding Brother's brand-new bike around the tree house. Brother was furious!

"That Fred!" growled Brother. "He can't do that!" And he charged outside.

"Uh-oh!" said Mama and Papa, running after him.

But they were too late. Brother was already chasing Fred around the tree house yelling for him to get off his bike. He startled Fred so much that poor Fred didn't look where he was going and ran right into the mailbox.

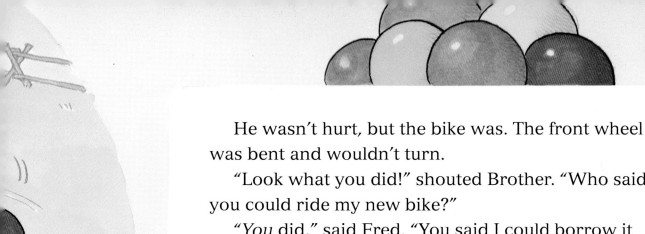

He wasn't hurt, but the bike was. The front wheel was bent and wouldn't turn.

"Look what you did!" shouted Brother. "Who said you could ride my new bike?"

"*You* did," said Fred. "You said I could borrow it anytime."

"I didn't mean right away," said Brother, stamping his feet. "I never even got to ride it!"

"Now Brother," said Mama, "calm down. This is just a misunderstanding. Fred didn't mean any harm."

"But my bike is ruined!" cried Brother. "Just look at it!"

"It's not ruined," said Papa. "We'll take it down to the bike shop and get it fixed up as good as new."

"But it won't be new!" said Brother. "It will never be brand-new again!" And he stormed off in a huff.

"Gee, I'm sorry," said Fred. He felt awful. "I never meant to hurt Brother or his new bike."

"Of course not, Fred," soothed Mama. "It was just an accident."

"I'm sorry Brother's so mad," said Fred. "Do you think he'll ever forgive me?"

"Of course he will," said Papa. "He'll get over it in no time."

But Sister wasn't so sure. She followed Brother to their backyard tree house.

"Mind if I come up?" she called. Brother didn't answer. Sister climbed the ladder and found Brother sitting, sulking, at the top.

"You're certainly in a good mood," said Sister.

"Humph!" grunted Brother.

Sister noticed a faded red line drawn down the middle of the tree house floor.

"Do you remember this red line?" she asked.

Brother shrugged.

"We put it there a long time ago," Sister went on. "We were so mad at each other that we divided the tree house in half. I sat on one side, and you sat on the other. We sat out here being mad at each other until it started to rain and we got soaked. By that time, we couldn't even remember what we were mad about."

"I guess so," said Brother.

As Brother and Sister sat in their tree house, it became cloudy and started to rain. They went back to the party and found the guests getting ready to break the piñata.

It was one Papa made in his workshop. There were all kinds of candies inside but especially licorice because licorice was Papa's favorite. Papa held the piñata out on a broomstick.

"Okay," he said. "Start swinging. But be careful not to hit *me*!"

One after another, the cubs whacked the piñata until it finally broke open, spilling candy onto the floor.

They all scrambled to grab some, including Papa. Brother scrambled right into Fred. In fact, they knocked heads.

"Ow!" said Fred, rubbing his noggin.

"Oops, sorry!" said Brother.

"That's okay, Brother," said Fred. "I forgive you."

"I forgive you too, Fred," said Brother, feeling ashamed of himself. "I shouldn't have yelled at you about the bike. It really was just an accident."

"Forget it," said Fred … and forget it they did as they gathered up the candy.

"You know," said Papa to Mama, as they watched the happy cubs, "that old tree in the backyard has seen a lot of forgiving over the years. I guess you'd call it a Forgiving Tree."

"As the Lord said," smiled Mama:
"And forgive us our debts, as we forgive
our debtors."

"What does that mean?" asked Sister.

"Just that God wants us to forgive those who hurt our feelings," said Mama.

"And, remember," added Papa, "though God wants us to be good, he forgives us when we do something wrong."

"Well, I think that's very nice of God," said Sister.
"Yes," agreed Mama and Papa, "it is!"